A BASKERVILLE CURSE

ANOTHER SHERLOCK HOLMES ALPHABET

By P. James Macaluso Jr.

Copyright

First edition published in 2019
© Copyright 2019
P. James Macaluso

Paperback ISBN 978-1-78705-515-5
ePub ISBN 978-1-78705-516-2
PDF ISBN 978-1-78705-517-9

Published by MX Publishing
335 Princess Park Manor, Royal Drive, London, N11 3GX
www.mxpublishing.com

Cover compiled by Brian Belanger

To Addy, my beloved hound,
or rather Spanish terrier.

Analysis

Baskerville Curse

Death Ensues

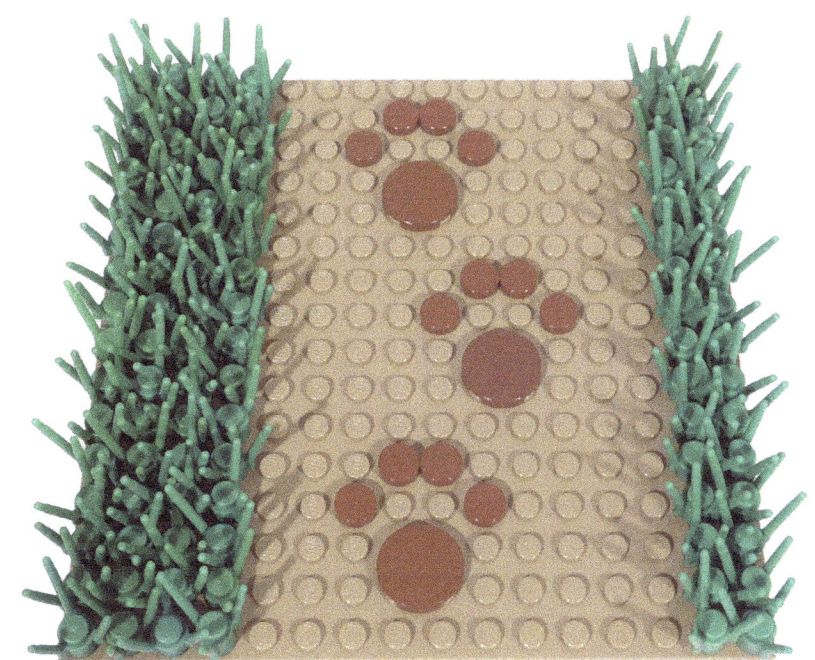

Footprints

Gigantic Hound

Investigation

Jeopardy

Keen Looker

Moor

Neighbours

Obscure Prisoner

Quagmire

Repeated Signals

Tor

Unmasking

Victim

Witness

eXpedition

Yowls

Zoothapsis

Notes on the text

A. The novel begins with Sherlock Holmes making a series of deductions concerning a walking stick that an unknown visitor has left behind at 221B Baker Street.

BC. In Chapter II, Dr Mortimer recounts the legend of the curse of the Baskervilles which began with the evil deeds of Sir Hugo in 1742.

DE. Dr Mortimer then proceeds to tell Sherlock Holmes about the recent and sudden death of Sir Charles at Baskerville Hall in Devonshire.

F. Dr Mortimer goes on to relate the odd circumstances connected with the death of Sir Charles Baskerville including footprints found some distance from the body.

GH. When Sherlock Holmes questions Dr Mortimer regarding the nature of the observed impressions, the latter exclaims that they were the footprints of a gigantic hound!

I. In Chapter III, Sherlock Holmes agrees to advise on the situation after hearing all the facts surrounding the death of Sir Charles and learning that his heir is due to arrive in London shortly.

J. In Chapter IV, Sherlock Holmes meets Sir Henry at which time the latter mentions a mysterious letter he received upon arriving in London warning him to keep away from the moor if he values his life and reason.

KL. Sherlock Holmes and Dr Watson trail Sir Henry when he leaves Baker Street as the detective suspects the young Baronet is being closely shadowed by someone, which proves to be the case as the two men set eyes on a stranger following Sir Henry in a Hansom cab.

M. In Chapter VI, following the suggestion of Sherlock Holmes, Dr Watson accompanies Sir Henry to Baskerville Hall on Dartmoor in Devonshire, when the young Baronet takes up residence in his ancestral home.

N. In Chapter VII, while taking a walk across the moor Dr Watson first meets, under odd circumstances, Jack Stapleton the naturalist and then his sister Beryl, who also live on Dartmoor.

OP. In Chapters VI and VIII, mention is made of an escaped convict from Princetown Gaol, the Notting Hill murderer, who we later learn is hiding upon the moor.

Q. In Chapter VII, Jack Stapleton warns Dr Watson of the dangers of the great Grippen Mire, a treacherous boggy area, where one false step could prove fatal.

RS. In Chapters VIII and IX, Dr Watson and Sir Henry observe, on several occasions, Barrymore the butler communicating by candlelight to someone out on the moor, which we later learn is Selden the escaped convict and brother of Mrs Barrymore.

T. In Chapter IX, Dr Watson and Sir Henry spot in the distance a stranger upon a tor, which we learn in Chapter XI is Sherlock Holmes, who has also been living on the moor and investigating the case from the shadows.

U. In Chapter XII, Sherlock Holmes reveals to Dr Watson that Jack Stapleton, who we later learn is a Baskerville himself, is responsible for the death of Sir Charles.

V. After hearing screams of horror out upon the moor, Sherlock Holmes and Dr Watson discover the body of Selden the convict, whom Stapleton mistakenly killed by setting the hound upon his track.

W. In Chapter XIII, Mrs Laura Lyons informs Sherlock Holmes that Stapleton, whom she loved, forced her to write the letter arranging the meeting at which Sir Charles died while fleeing in fear from the hound.

X. In Chapter XIV, after setting a trap, Sherlock Holmes, Dr Watson and Inspector Lestrade, who has been summoned from London, wait outside Stapleton's house to catch him red-handed in an attack on Sir Henry.

Y. After dining with the Stapletons, Sir Henry walks home across the moor, at which time he is attacked by the hound which lets out several howls while being shot and killed by Sherlock Holmes and Dr Watson.

Z. The next day Mrs Stapleton reveals the pathway to the center of Grippen Mire, the location of her husband's hideout, but there is no sign of Jack Stapleton and he is presumed to have fallen into the boggy waters during his hasty flight the night before, thus being buried alive.

Other books by the author

A SHELROCK HOLMES ALPHABET: Selected characters and objects featuring in the Sherlock Holmes stories written by Arthur Conan Doyle are presented in rhyming verse, from A to Z, and accompanied by amusing photographic illustrations of custom designed LEGO® models and minifigures.

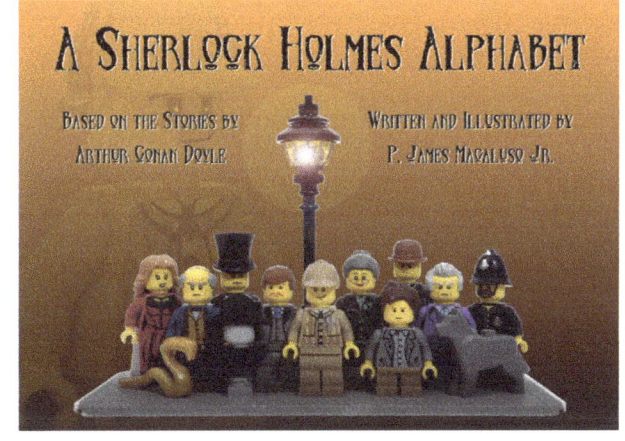

Other books by the author

SHERLOCK HOLMES RE-IMAGINED: The original Sherlock Holmes stories delightfully illustrated using only LEGO® minifigures and bricks. There are 13 individual books in the series, as well as a complete edition that combines the first 12 stories into a single volume.

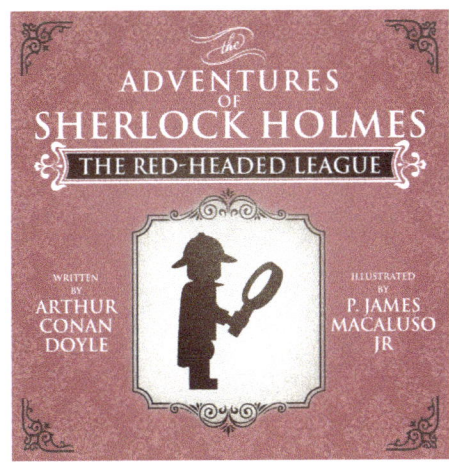

Other books by the author

THE LEGEND OF SLEEPY HOLLOW RE-IMAGINED: The original and unabridged text of Washington Irving's ghostly tale accompanied by twenty-eight charming color photographic illustrations featuring custom designed models built using only LEGO® brand minifigures and bricks.

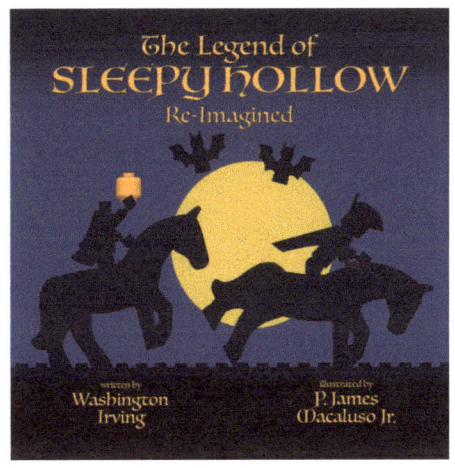